T0381335

Little Thunder's First Sound

TONI WITHANEYE

AuthorHouse™
1663 Liberty Drive
Bloomington, IN 47403
www.authorhouse.com
Phone: 833-262-8899

Because of the dynamic nature of the Internet, any web addresses or links contained in this book may have changed
since publication and may no longer be valid. The views expressed in this work are solely those of the author and do not
necessarily reflect the views of the publisher, and the publisher hereby disclaims any responsibility for them.

Any people depicted in stock imagery provided by Getty Images are models,
and such images are being used for illustrative purposes only.
Certain stock imagery © Getty Images.

This book is printed on acid-free paper.

ISBN: 978-1-4634-1576-1 (sc)
ISBN: 978-1-4817-1508-9 (e)

Library of Congress Control Number: 2011910309

Print information available on the last page.

Published by AuthorHouse 11/11/2021

authorHOUSE

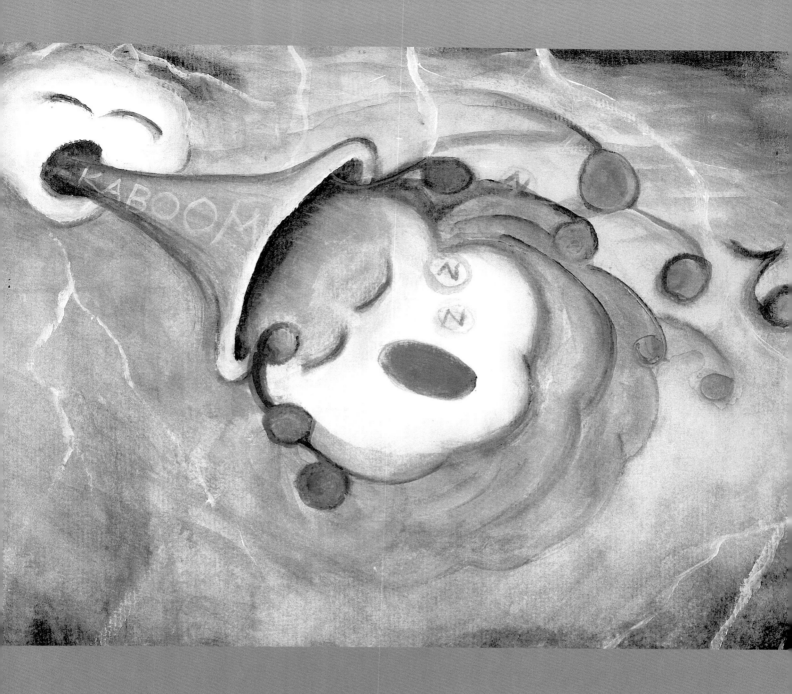

Little Thunder was asleep in the clouds. Big Thunder could be heard for miles around.

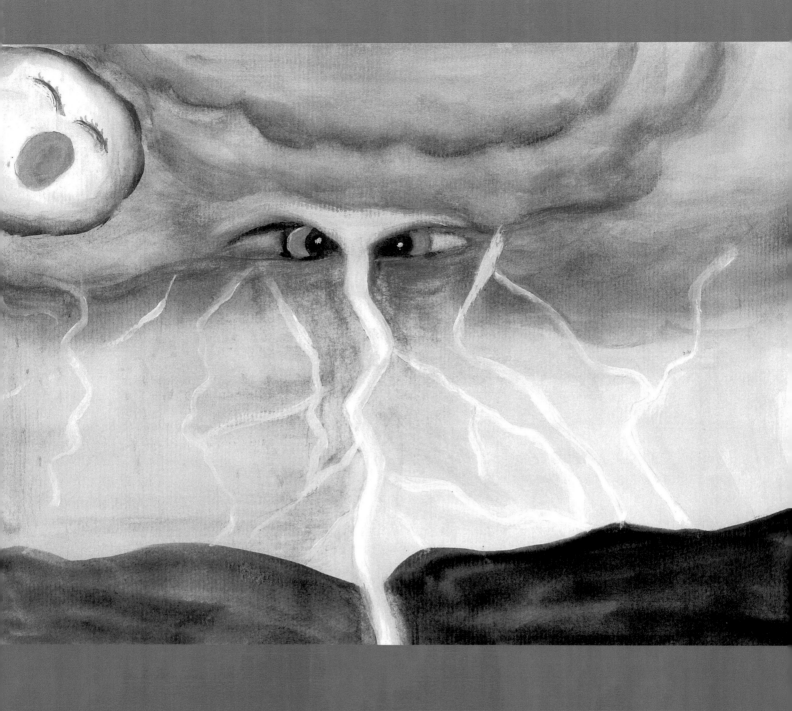

Bright Lighting was always ready to shine, with a flash of light he hits the ground!

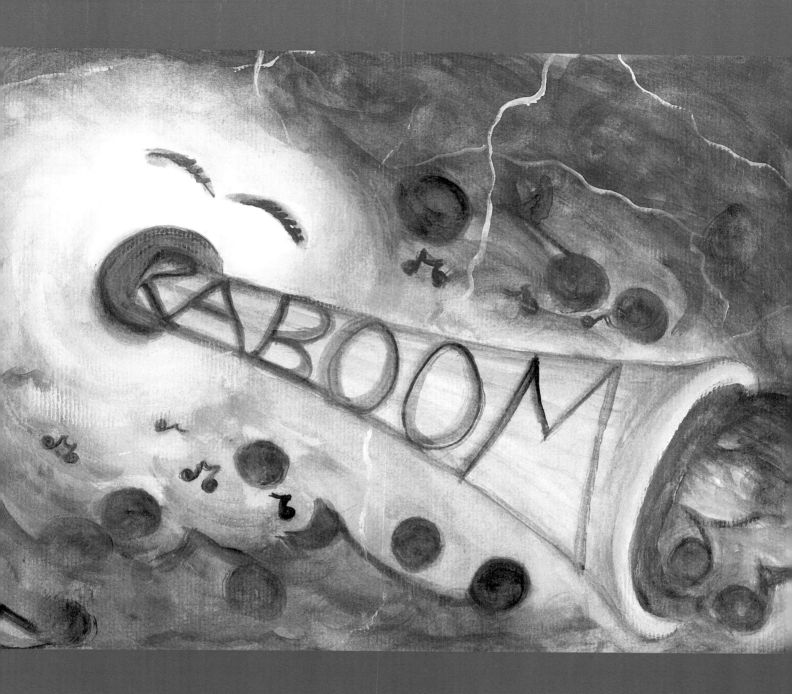

Just in time as loud as he could, Big Thunder let loose. "KABOOM! KABOOM! KABOOM!" Little Thunder listened as he should.

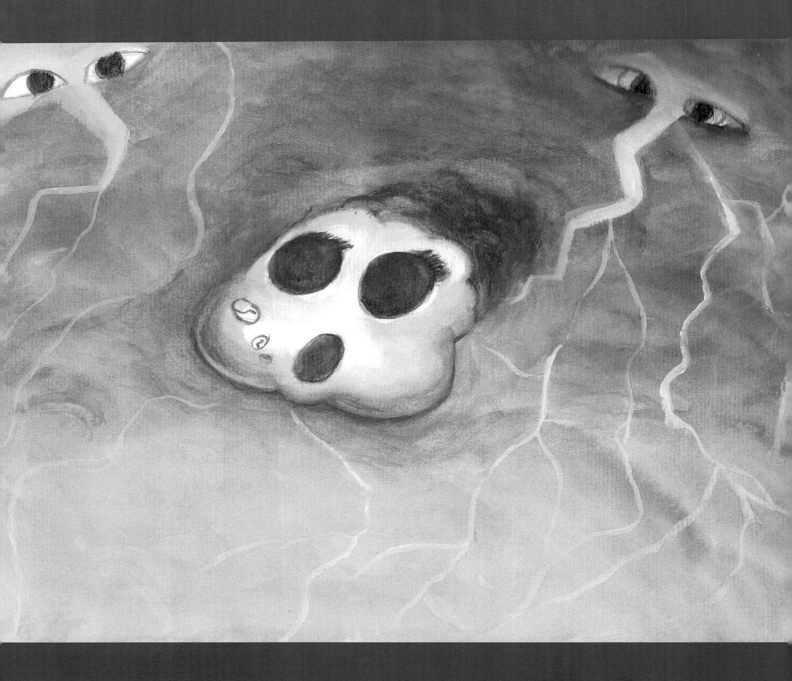

Little Thunder knew it was his turn to
"KABOOM!" But for some reason he could
not play that tune. Little Thunder was afraid of
making too much noise and scaring little girls
and boys.

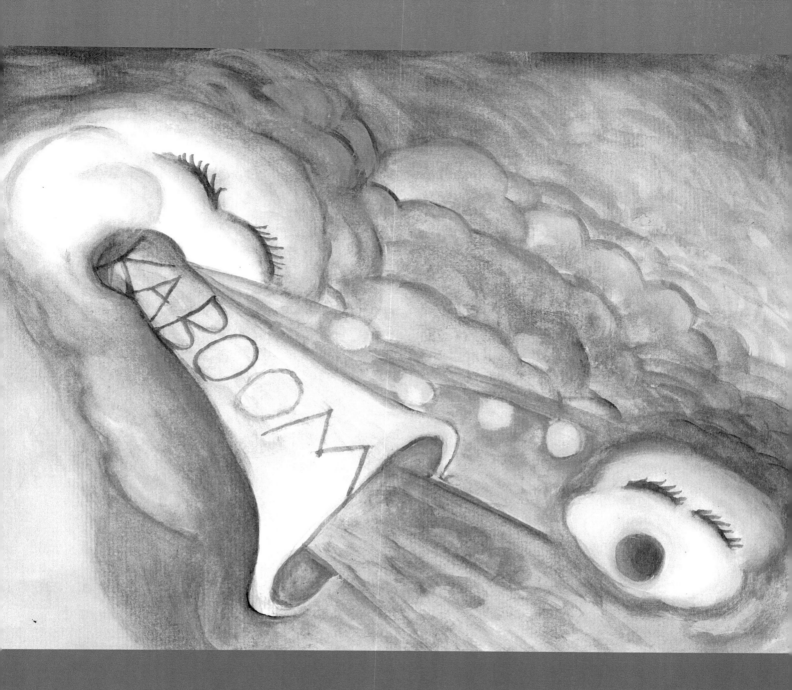

"KABOOM! KABOOM!" Big Thunder
explained, "our voices must be heard especially
when it rains."

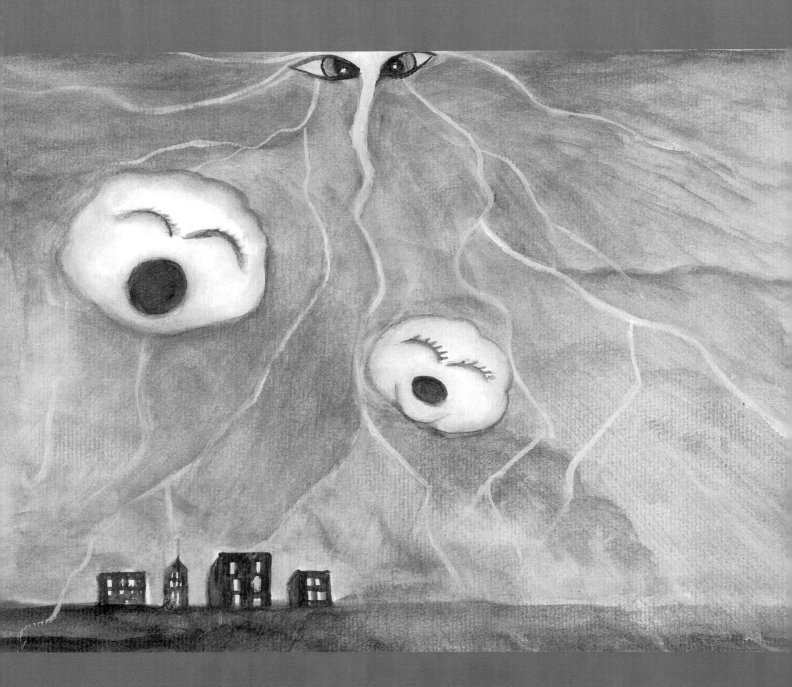

The "KABOOM" concerned Little Thunder. But Big Thunder said "we are giving a warning from the clouds. When lighting flashes, we become very loud. Everyone on the ground will hear the sound and get out the way before lighting reaches their town."

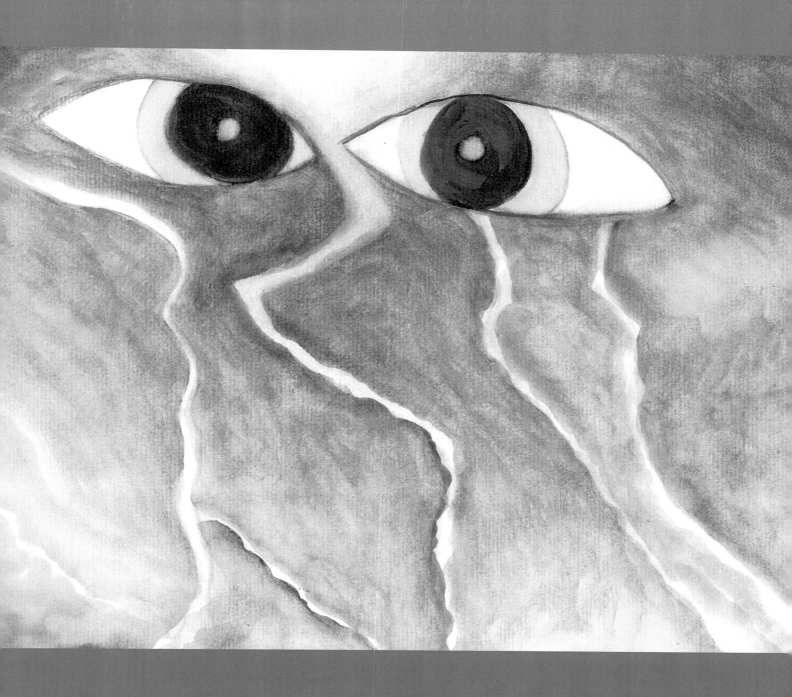

"FLASH!" Bright Lighting was glowing and fast.
Little Thunder was now ready for the task.

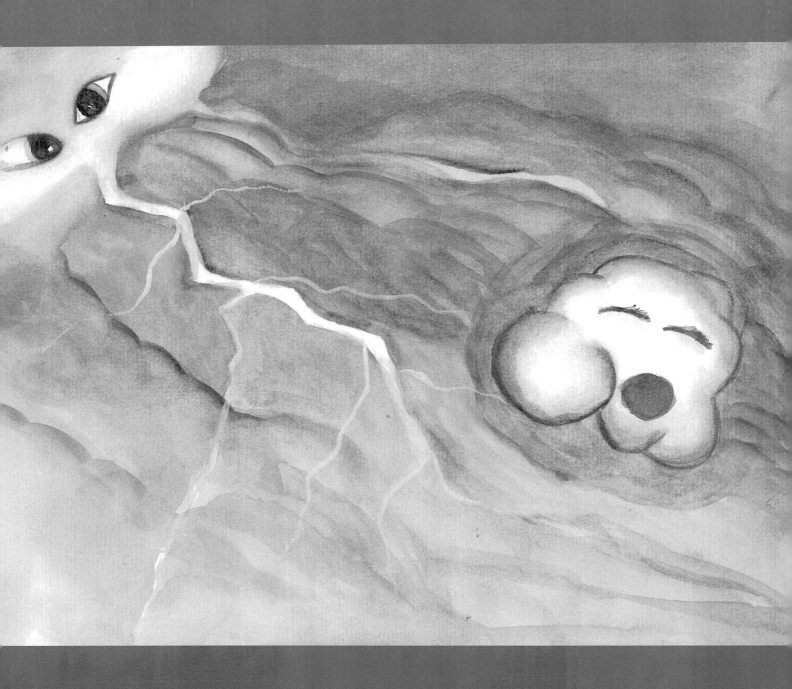

"FLASH! FLASH!" Bright Lighting had sent a
flare. Huffing and puffing Little Thunder filled
with air.

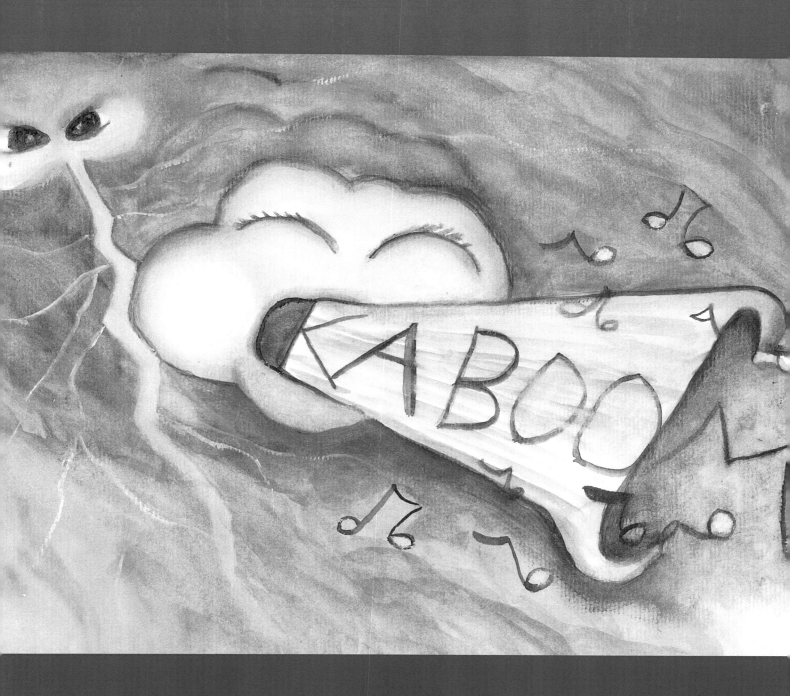

"KABOOM!" Could be heard everywhere.

Little Thunder played his first sound.

He was happy to warn the little children
on the ground.

Mrs. Toni, as she is known to her students, continues to delight children with her story adventures. She is also the author and illustrator of *Moon Jumping Babies*. Toni loves to spend time with her family in Florida. You can visit her online at www.toniwithaneye.com.